Sometimes, if I can, take a shower instead of a bath.

Try to remember to turn the TV or computer off completely —and absolutely never EVER leave them on standby.

Make presents and birthday cards for my friends from knickknacks around the house.

Try not to beg Mum and Dad for the latest and most extremely good new toy—and donate some of my birthday or Christmas money to charity instead. (This might be really hard to do, so you definitely deserve an extra-big well done.)

characters created by

# lauren child

We are
**Extremely** VERY
Good
**Recyclers**

dial books for young readers

# Charlie <3 and Lola™

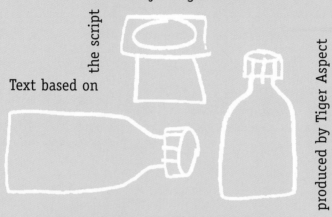

written by Bridget Hurst

the script

Text based on

produced by Tiger Aspect

Illustrations from the TV animation

First published in the United States by
DIAL BOOKS FOR YOUNG READERS
A division of Penguin Young Readers Group
Published by The Penguin Group
Penguin Group (USA) Inc., 375 Hudson Street, New York, NY 10014, U.S.A.
Penguin Group (Canada), 90 Eglinton Avenue East, Suite 700, Toronto, Ontario, Canada M4P 2Y3 (a division of Pearson Penguin Canada Inc.)
Penguin Books Ltd, 80 Strand, London WC2R 0RL, England
Penguin Ireland, 25 St. Stephen's Green, Dublin 2, Ireland (a division of Penguin Books Ltd)
Penguin Group (Australia), 250 Camberwell Road, Camberwell, Victoria 3124, Australia (a division of Pearson Australia Group Pty Ltd)
Penguin Books India Pvt Ltd, 11 Community Centre, Panchsheel Park, New Delhi - 110 017, India
Penguin Group (NZ), 67 Apollo Drive, Rosedale, North Shore, New Zealand (a division of Pearson New Zealand Ltd)
Penguin Books (South Africa) (Pty) Ltd, 24 Sturdee Avenue, Rosebank, Johannesburg 2196, South Africa
Penguin Books Ltd, Registered Offices: 80 Strand, London WC2R 0RL, England

Published in Great Britain as *Look After Your Planet* by Puffin Books
Copyright © 2009 by Lauren Child/Tiger Aspect Productions Limited
The Charlie and Lola logo is a trademark of Lauren Child and Tiger Aspect Productions Limited

Manufactured in China on acid-free recycled paper
3  5  7  9  10  8  6  4  2
Library of Congress Cataloging-in-Publication Data
Child, Lauren.
We are extremely very good recyclers / characters created by Lauren Child ; [text based on the script written by Bridget Hurst ; illustrations from the TV animation produced by Tiger Aspect].
p.  cm.
ISBN 978-0-8037-3335-0
I. Hurst, Bridget. II. Tiger Aspect Productions. III. Charlie and Lola (Television program) IV. Title.
PZ7.C4383Lo 2009
[E]—dc22
2008010002

I have this little sister Lola.
She is small and very funny.
Lola loves keeping things. All kinds of things.
Boxes, old broken toys . . . just things.

"Not anymore!"
    says Lola.

    I say,
"Has it got anything
        to do with when
we went to Marv's house?"

And Lola says,
    "Mmm, maybe . . ."

Yesterday, Marv says,
"I dare **anyone** to go into my
big brother Marty's room.
He doesn't let anyone touch any of his things
and he won't throw anything away.
Mum says his room looks like
a complete pigsty."

I say, "He can't be that bad."

When we sneak into
Marty's bedroom,
Lola says,
    "Ooh, it's stinky."

But then we hear,
"Get out
    of my
    room!
      . . . NOW!!"

And Marv shouts,
    "Run!"

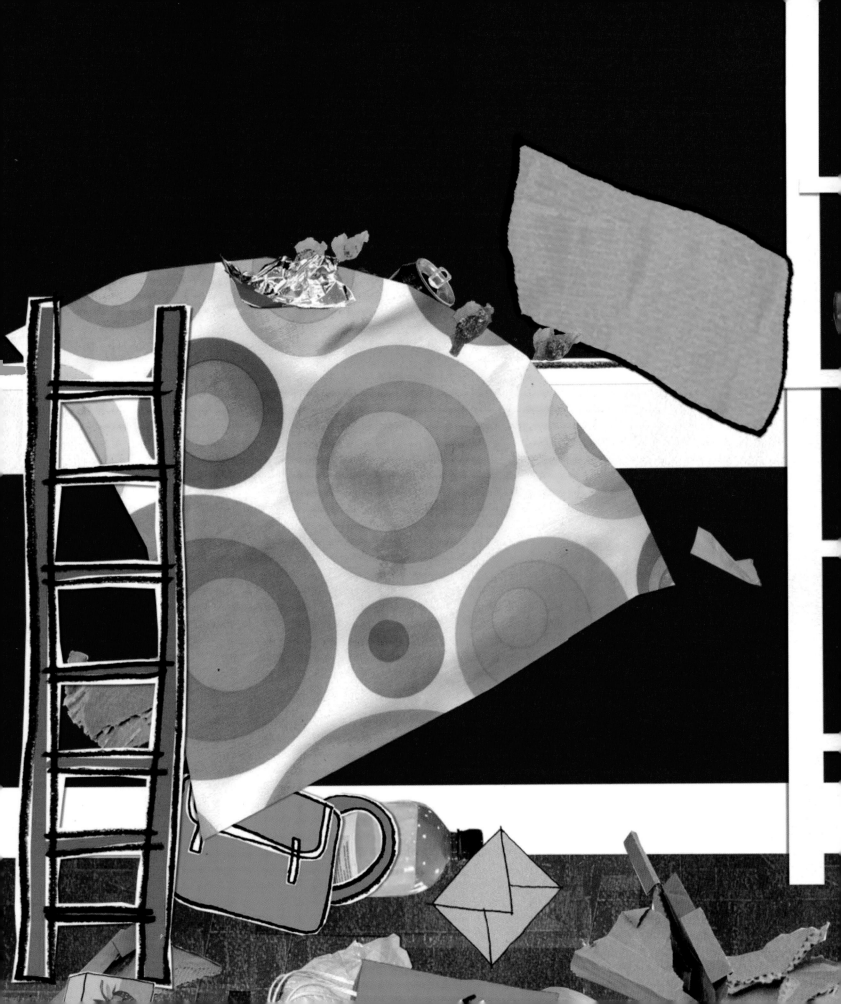

"So you see, Charlie,
        I do not ever, never want my room to
look like Marty's. So I am throwing everything
away.
        Because I do not need it."

"Why don't you recycle it?"

And Lola says,
        "Bicycle it?"

"No, **re**-cycle it."

"Recycle it? What is that?" says Lola.

"Well, it's a way
that people can **reuse**
OLD things in a different
and NEW-ish way."

"Why?" says Lola.

"Because if we throw everything
        away, then we will all be
completely buried under a

massive, **huge** pile of garbage.

"And if we don't use things again, in the end we will just run out of everything.

So recycling is a good idea.

Did you know there are
these places where they make
NEW paper out of OLD paper?

The OLD paper gets
smooshed up with
water and things.

And then they
press it all flat.

"Then they make all sorts of NEW types of paper, like . . .

writing paper,

toilet paper,

wrapping paper,

and coloring-in

egg  cartons,

paper."

"That is clever," says Lola.

Later Lola says,
"Look, Charlie!
Mum bought me this special comic book.
It's called

# Look after YOUR Planet

and there's lots about recycling in it."

And I say, "Ooh! A contest. You can win a tree all your own to plant."

"What do we have to do?" says Lola.

"We have to collect a hundred of each thing.

One hundred tin cans,

one hundred plastic things

and one hundred things made out of paper."

"That's a lot of things," says Lola.

"Look, Lola! Your very own tree counter.

"Every time you collect
          something to recycle
you can stick a leaf
          onto a branch.
When your tree counter
          is completely filled up
you can get your very own
          real tree to plant."

Lola says,
"I would love to plant a tree."

"Well, you'd better
start recycling."

And Lola says,
          "OK, Charlie!

This
     box

is for

     all the

plastic

     things

and

**this**

one

is for

**tin**

cans

and

**this**

one

is for

**paper.**

And I have
        already recycled
two plastic
            things,
two baked bean cans,
        and some paper."

I say, "I'm not sure we will be able to collect a hundred of each thing in just two weeks, Lola, all on our own."

And Lola says,
"Of course we can, Charlie.
Have you finished?
Good . . ."

Later Lola says,
"See, Charlie! I can recycle these
toilet paper rolls."

And I say, "The idea is to use the
paper really slowly and not waste it—
so we don't have to cut down lots of trees!
Then you recycle the rolls."

"Well, we need some
more leaves on
our tree counter.
So maybe we
need to ask
even more people."

The next day at school,
     Lola says,
"We have to save the trees and stop
     us being covered in a **big**
          **large** pile of
                    **garbage.**

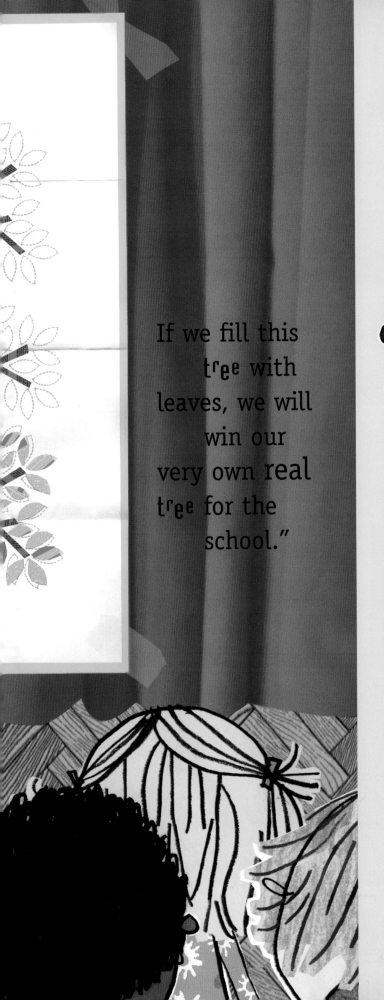

If we fill this tree with leaves, we will win our very own real tree for the school."

Everyone is excited and says,

"I want to do recycling . . . pass it on."

"I want to do recycling . . . pass it on."

"I want to do recycling . . . pass it on."

So everyone at school starts **recycling**.

"Look how many I've got!"

"I've got lots too!"

"You are a **very** good **recycler**, Lotta!"

"Oh, Morten, you're not helping."

So Morten goes home . . .

. . . and he finds more things to recycle.

When everything is **recycled**,
Lola says,
"Oh no. We have NOT
filled up the
**whole** t**r**ee . . .
so we will NOT be
getting our
own **real** t**r**ee."

But then Morten
comes along.

Lotta says,

"**Look** at
what he's
**GOT!**"

And soon . . .

Then Marv whispers to Morten,
"Where did you get all that?"

And Morten says,
"Marty's bedroom."

Marv says,
"You are going
to be in
SUCH
big
trouble."

The next day
    we all go outside
to **plant** the tree.

"Look! Our very own real school tree!" says Lola.
"We are extremely very good
recyclers, aren't we!"

Later, when we are all
at Marv's, we suddenly hear,

"Who's
been in
my
ROOM?"

"Let's get out of here!" says Marv.
And Morten says,
"Quick! Run for it!"

Here are some MORE especially good promises
to help you
Look after YOUR Planet:

I REALLY ever so definitely promise to:

☐ Try to maybe sometimes ride my bicycle
or walk to school if I can.

☐ Remember to shut all the doors
when I'm inside to keep in the heat.

☐ Encourage absolutely all my friends,
parents, and next-door people
to reuse plastic bags.